W9-AEA-525

Perfectly POPPY

Poppy's New Puppy

Story by Michele Jakubowski

Pictures by Erica-Jane Waters

Picture Window Books

Perfectly Poppy is published by Picture Window Books, a Capstone Imprint
1710 Roe Crest Drive, North Mankato, MN 56003
www.capstonepub.com

Library of Congress Cataloging-in-Publication Data
Jakubowski, Michele, author.
Poppy's puppy / by Michele Jakubowski ; illustrated by Erica-Jane Waters.
pages cm -- (Perfectly Poppy)
Summary: When Poppy's parents finally let her adopt a puppy from the shelter, Poppy discovers
that there is a lot of responsibility and work involved in a puppy, but fortunately her best
friend, Millie, is there to help.
ISBN 978-1-4795-5799-8 (hardcover) -- ISBN 978-1-4795-5803-2 (pbk.)
ISBN 978-1-4795-6201-5 (ebook pdf)
1. Puppies--Juvenile fiction. 2. Pet adoption--Juvenile fiction. 3. Responsibility--Juvenile
fiction. 4. Best friends--Juvenile fiction. [1. Dogs--Fiction. 2. Pet adoption--Fiction. 3.
Responsibility--Fiction. 4. Best friends--Fiction. 5. Friendship--Fiction.] I. Waters, Erica-Jane,
illustrator. II. Title. III. Series: Jakubowski, Michele. Perfectly Poppy.
PZ7.J153555Pop 2015
813.6--dc23   2014015331

Image credits: Shutterstock
Designer: Kristi Carlson

Printed in China by Nordica
0914/CA21401511
092014   008470NORDS15

Table of Contents

Chapter 1
A Fluffy Puppy

"That's the one!" Poppy shouted. She was pointing at a fluffy, white puppy.

Poppy had wanted a puppy for a long time. She had asked her parents for one every day. On her birthday, they had finally said yes! Poppy was thrilled.

"Are you sure that's the one you want?" Poppy's mom asked.

Poppy put her face near the cage. The puppy licked her.

"Yes, I'm sure!" Poppy said.

Poppy's dad took the puppy
out of its cage. He placed it in
Poppy's arms. Poppy had never
been so happy!

"Now remember, Poppy,

puppies need a lot of attention,"

her dad said.

"I know," Poppy said. She

hugged the little ball of fur in her

arms. "We'll play together every

single day!"

"Do you have a name picked out?" Poppy's mom asked.

"Rosie," Poppy said. "Her name is Rosie."

Chapter 2

Rosie Rules

A few days later, Poppy and her best friend, Mille, were trying to watch their favorite TV show. But Rosie was making that hard to do. She kept jumping and barking.

"Quiet, Rosie!" Poppy said.

Just then, Poppy's mom came into the room.

"Rosie wants to play," she said. "Puppies have a lot of energy. They need plenty of activity. Why don't you girls take her out in the yard?"

"Fine," Poppy said, but she wasn't happy about it.

She turned off the TV. She didn't like missing her favorite TV show, but she had promised to take care of Rosie.

When they got outside, Poppy

and Millie sat on the ground.

Rosie danced around them.

"What do you play with her?"

Millie asked.

"I don't know," Poppy said.
"I've tried lots of games, but she
doesn't know how to play any
of them."

Poppy threw a ball into the yard. Rosie barked and chased after it. A short while later she came back to Poppy without the ball.

"See?" Poppy asked. "She never brings it back."

"I guess she has her own rules," Millie said.

"She has Rosie rules," Poppy said, laughing.

Millie thought for a moment. "Maybe she doesn't know that you want her to bring it back."

"You're right!" Poppy jumped

to her feet. "We need to teach her!"

Chapter 3
Good Girl

"You throw the ball, and I'll go get it," Poppy said to Millie.

"Okay," Millie said. She threw the ball far into the yard.

"Let's go, Rosie!" Poppy

shouted. She ran after the ball.

Rosie ran beside her.

When they got to the ball,

Poppy said, "Pick it up, Rosie!"

Rosie looked up at Poppy

and barked. She did not pick up

the ball.

"Like this," Poppy said. She picked up the ball. Rosie jumped up to get it from Poppy.

"Yes! Now you're getting it," Poppy said.

She let Rosie put the ball in her mouth. She tried to get it back, but Rosie held on tight.

"Rosie, drop the ball," Poppy said. To her surprise, Rosie dropped the ball.

"She's getting it!" Millie said.

"Good girl, Rosie," Poppy said.

"Let's try throwing it again,"

Millie said. "This time I'll chase

after it with Rosie."

Poppy, Millie, and Rosie ran

around the yard chasing the ball.

They had so much fun!

"How about a snack break?"

Poppy's mom called.

Poppy and Millie sat at the

kitchen table munching on apples.

"Good news! I think Rosie finally knows how to play fetch," Poppy told her mom.

"It must be a lot of hard work learning a new game," Poppy's mom said.

Poppy and Millie looked under the table. Rosie was curled up on the floor sound asleep.

"It sure is!" they laughed.

Poppy's New Words

I learned so many new words today! I made sure to write them down so I could use them again.

activity (ak-TIV-uh-tee) — action or movement

attention (uh-TEN-shuhn) — special care or treatment

energy (EN-ur-jee) — ability to do active things without getting tired

promised (PROM-isst) — gave your word that you would do something

shelter (SHEL-tur) — a place that provides food and protection for people or animals that need help

Poppy's Ponders

After Rosie fell asleep, I had some time to think. Here are some of my questions and thoughts from the day.

1. I love my new puppy. If you could have any pet in the world, what would it be and why?

2. I was surprised that Rosie had so much energy. When you have lots of energy, what do you like to do?

3. I had to teach Rosie how to play fetch. Write about a time when you taught someone something.

4. Having a puppy is a lot of work. Write a list of at least three things you have to do to take care of a pet.

Game Time!

I played fetch with Rosie, but there are lots of different games to play with a dog. If you don't have a dog, play these games with a friend. Be sure to reward your dog when he/she does something the right way. If you want, you can reward your friend, too.

Blanket Hurdles

Make an obstacle course by using blankets or towels. Just roll up your blankets or towels and show your dog how to jump over them. If you are playing with a friend, you can time each other.

Simon Says

If your dog knows the basic commands of sit, stay, down, roll over, and shake, this game is for you! Test your dog's listening skills by calling out the commands. If you are playing with a friend, be sure to actually say "Simon says," which you won't say when playing with your pup.

Grab your dog's favorite ball and a laundry basket. Show your dog how to drop the ball into the basket when you say "drop." It might take a few tries, but your dog will soon understand how to make a basket. If you are playing with a friend, see who can make the most shots. Make it fun by doing silly tricks like turning in circles before you shoot or shooting with your eyes closed.

About the Author

Raised in the Chicago suburb of Hoffman Estates, Michele Jakubowski has the teachers in her life to thank for her love of reading and writing. While writing has always been a passion for Michele, she believes it is the books she has read throughout the years, and the teachers who assigned them, that have made her the storyteller she is today. Michele lives in Powell, Ohio, with her husband, John, and their children, Jack and Mia.

About the Illustrator

Erica-Jane Waters grew up in the beautiful Northern Irish countryside, where her imagination was ignited by the local folklore and fairytales. She now lives in Oxfordshire, England, with her young family. Erica writes and illustrates children's books and creates art for magazines, greeting cards, and various other projects.